The BOY and the GHOST

by Robert D. San Souci
illustrated by J. Brian Pinkney

Aladdin Paperbacks

For Sean Martin
whose friendship has always
meant so much

—R.D.S.

To my mother and father

—J.B.P.

Aladdin Paperbacks
An imprint of Simon & Schuster
Children's Publishing Division
1230 Avenue of the Americas
New York, NY 10020
Text copyright © 1989 by Robert San Souci
Illustrations copyright © 1989 by J. Brian Pinkney

Printed in Hong Kong

10 9 8 7 6 5

Library of Congress Cataloging-in-Publication Data

San Souci, Robert D.
The boy and the ghost / by Robert San Souci ;
illustrated by J. Brian Pinkney. p.   cm.
SUMMARY: A poor boy hopes to win a fortune for himself
and his family by spending the night in a haunted house
and bravely standing up to a frightening ghost.
[1. Ghosts—Fiction.   2. Haunted houses—Fiction.]
I. Pinkney, J. Brian, Ill.   II. Title.
PZ7.S1947Bo   1989   [E]—dc19   89-4185   CIP   AC

ISBN: 0-671-79248-2

The Boy and the Ghost

Down south, there was once a boy named Thomas whose
family was very poor. His parents worked hard from sunup
to sundown on their little backcountry farm, but could barely
put enough food on the table to feed their seven children.
Thomas had two brothers and a sister older than he was,
and two sisters and a brother who were younger, so he was
right smack in the middle.

Because he hated to see his parents work so hard, and his brothers and sisters go hungry all the time, the boy made up his mind to go to the city to earn some money, so he could bring it back and help his family.

Since the older children had to help their parents chop cotton, and the younger ones were too little to go off on their own, Thomas, in the middle, decided *he* ought to be the one to try and help in this way.

He set out the next morning. His mother hugged him and gave him a pot and a hambone to make soup and said, "Now, you always be polite to anyone you meet, and generous as well."

Then his father embraced the boy, gave him a box of matches and a croaker-sack to carry things in, and told Thomas, "Be brave, no matter what happens, and always be honest."

"We'll miss you!" cried his three sisters and three brothers, and they hugged him one and all.

"I'll miss you, too," said Thomas, putting on a brave smile to hide how sad he felt at leaving. So, off he went.

As he walked along the road that led to the city, he picked up sticks for a fire. And he found some greens and other good things that grew wild, and put these in his croaker-sack.

When he stopped for lunch, he lit a fire. Then he filled his pot with fresh water from a stream and added the hambone and the things he had gathered. Soon he had some soup boiling away nicely.

When he was ready to eat, a poor man came by, even more raggedy than Thomas, and asked, "Can I have just a taste of that soup?"

"Of course," said the little boy, politely inviting the raggedy man to dip his tin cup into the broth. Together, they finished the soup, and tasty it was.

When they were done, the man said, "Where're you heading, boy?"

"To the city to earn money so's I can help my family," he answered.

"You mightn't have to go so far," said the other, "if you're brave enough.

"I hear there's a house on a hill not far from here. A rich man lived there years ago, but he died. Folks say the place's haunted. But the same folks say anyone who stays in it from sunset to sunrise will get the house and the treasure the old man hid before he died."

"Why don't you go and get the treasure yourself?" Thomas asked.

"I'm scared—that's the long 'n' short of it. Folks say everyone who's tried to last the night has run away or died of fright. Now, no one'll go near the place."

Thomas thought of his poor family at home.

"*I* will," he said, gathering up his hambone and pot, and putting them in his croaker-sack.

Soon after, boy and man parted company. Just before sunset, Thomas spotted the lonely old house on the hill.

Bravely, he walked up and pushed open the door with a *Scriiiitch!*

Inside, most of the dusty rooms and cobwebby hallways were empty. But, in the kitchen, he found a big old iron stove opposite a fireplace. There were also a table with one chair, a candle and a spoon.

The boy lit the candle. Then he put the last of his kindling in the stove, drew some water from a well outside the back door, and put in the hambone and remaining greens to make soup for his supper.

While it was warming, a bright light suddenly filled the fireplace across the room. There was an awful moan. Then a thin, sad voice wailed down the chimney, "Look out, my legs are falling!"

With a *Whoomp!* a pair of legs encased in elegant trousers, starting at fine leather shoes and ending at a wide belt with a gold buckle, dropped into the ashes in the cold fireplace.

Immediately, they got up and began running around the kitchen. They kicked at walls and doors and even the side of the big iron stove, so Thomas had to keep moving out of their way.

"Aren't you going to run away?" asked the ghostly voice.

"I'm fine right where I am, just so's you don't kick over my soup," Thomas said, stirring the boiling pot.

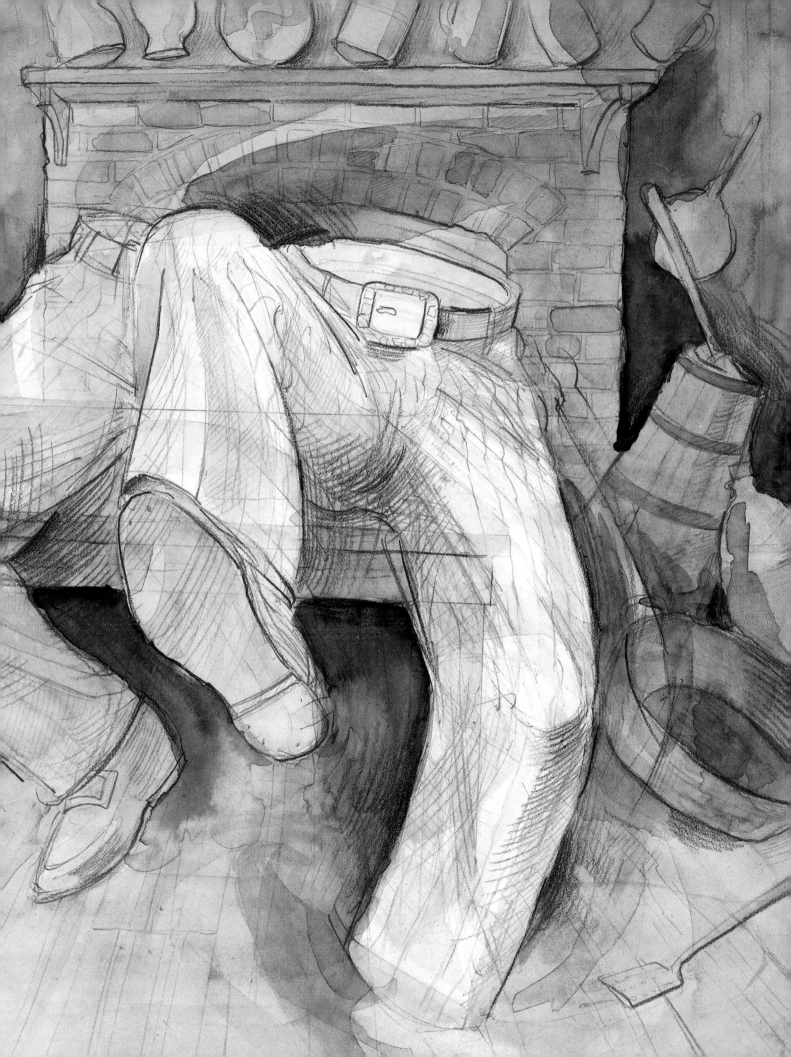

Just as he was ready to carry his soup to the table, the voice wailed down the chimney, "Look out, my arms are falling!"

And, with a *Whump!* a man's two arms and middle, clothed in a silken shirt with silver buttons, dropped into the fireplace. Immediately, the legs went over and stood waiting, while the other part climbed up and settled in place. Then the headless body fumbled around the kitchen, rattling cupboards and pounding on walls.

"Aren't you going to run away?" the strange voice called down the chimney.

But Thomas, who was sitting at the table, dipping up his broth with the spoon, answered, "No need to. Just see that you don't knock over my soup."

"Look out!" warned the voice, "Here comes the rest of me!"

Then a scowling head, with hair and beard red as flame and eyes like blazing coals, dropped *Thunk!* into the fireplace ashes.

Right away the body of the man, or ghost, or whatever it was, picked up the head from the hearth, brushed it off, and set it squarely on its shoulders.

"Now," roared the figure, hands on hips, "what do you say?"

"Do you want some soup?" asked Thomas, who wouldn't let his courage or his manners fail him. "There's still a little left in the pot, and you're welcome to share it."

The ghostly figure said, "I don't need any food. But you're the only one, man or boy, who's stayed long enough for me to put myself together. Now, follow me." He raised his left hand. Immediately, his fingers blazed like a torch, though the fire didn't seem to hurt him any. "Now fetch the shovel that's out by the well, and follow me—if you dare!"

"I will," said Thomas.

The ghost led the little boy to a lonely spot far from
the house. Stopping under a huge sycamore tree, the ghost
pointed with his right hand to the ground near its roots.
"Dig there," he commanded.

Thomas dug and dug, until the shovel fell from his
blistered hands. The ghost remained silent, one hand raised
and glowing, the finger of his other hand still pointing to
the hole.

After a short rest, Thomas wearily began digging again.
Soon the point of his shovel struck something hard. He
uncovered a large earthen pot caked with dirt. When he lifted
the lid, he saw gold and silver coins shining in the first glow
of sunrise.

"Give half my money to the poor, so my soul can rest
easy," said the ghost, as his legs faded away, "and keep half for
yourself." His arms and middle disappeared up to his neck.

"You're a good, brave lad," added the floating head, with
a wink. "You set me free, and I thank you."

"You're—" Thomas began, but the head was gone before
he could say, "welcome."

Thomas did as he was told. He loaded the gold and silver into his croaker-sack. On his way home, he gave half the money away to poor folk.

When he got back to the farm, his family was overjoyed to have him back safe and sound. Then the boy shared his wealth with the rest of his family, and they all moved into the house on the hill and lived happily ever after. And the ghost was never seen again in those parts.

The idea for this story and many of the plot details came from two very brief "negro ghost stories" originally written down around the turn of the century. One was from the western part of Virginia and one, from southern Alabama; both were first printed in the *Southern Workman and Hampton School Record*, March, 1898, and reprinted in the *Journal of American Folk-Lore*, 1906.

When working with folktales, however, one very often finds that a story set in one locale may actually be a new version of a much older tale that has traveled a great distance. On its journey, the narrative may have undergone many changes as now this, now the other storyteller told it his or her way, perhaps giving it a local setting or adding new incidents.

But, when one looks closely, one can still find the echoes of much older tales. So it is with *The Boy and the Ghost*. The basic plot of a boy or man visiting a haunted house or castle and meeting up with a ghost "bit by bit" turns up many times in world folk literature. Tales of this sort have been told in Spain, on Mallorca, in the British Isles, in Germany (where the Brothers Grimm retold a version of it), and in other countries.

The notion that ghosts often watch over hidden treasure turns up again and again in folktales around the world—from ancient Chinese accounts to the popular stories set in the American West about ghosts that guard the lost gold mines. The *Southern Workman and Hampton School Record* (as reported in the *Journal of American Folk-Lore*) noted, "The ghost in negro folk-lore is a being often misunderstood. If met with courage, he rewards those who speak to him, as he is in many cases the guardian of concealed treasure."

Very likely, the tale of a hero and a ghost who appears a little at a time traveled from the Old World to the New with colonists and immigrants, and was handed down (as good stories are) as a legacy to sons and daughters growing up under very different circumstances. As they, in turn, shared it with new listeners in a new land, the haunted European castle was changed to a haunted plantation house in the American South, and the brash Spanish tinker became a brave little boy. Gradually, the story took on a fresh new feel and became part of American folk literature.

Robert San Souci